ONE
SILLY
SAUSAGE
DOG

For Tips, a silly but
very good dog. – A.C.

For Nash and Peter. – A.W.

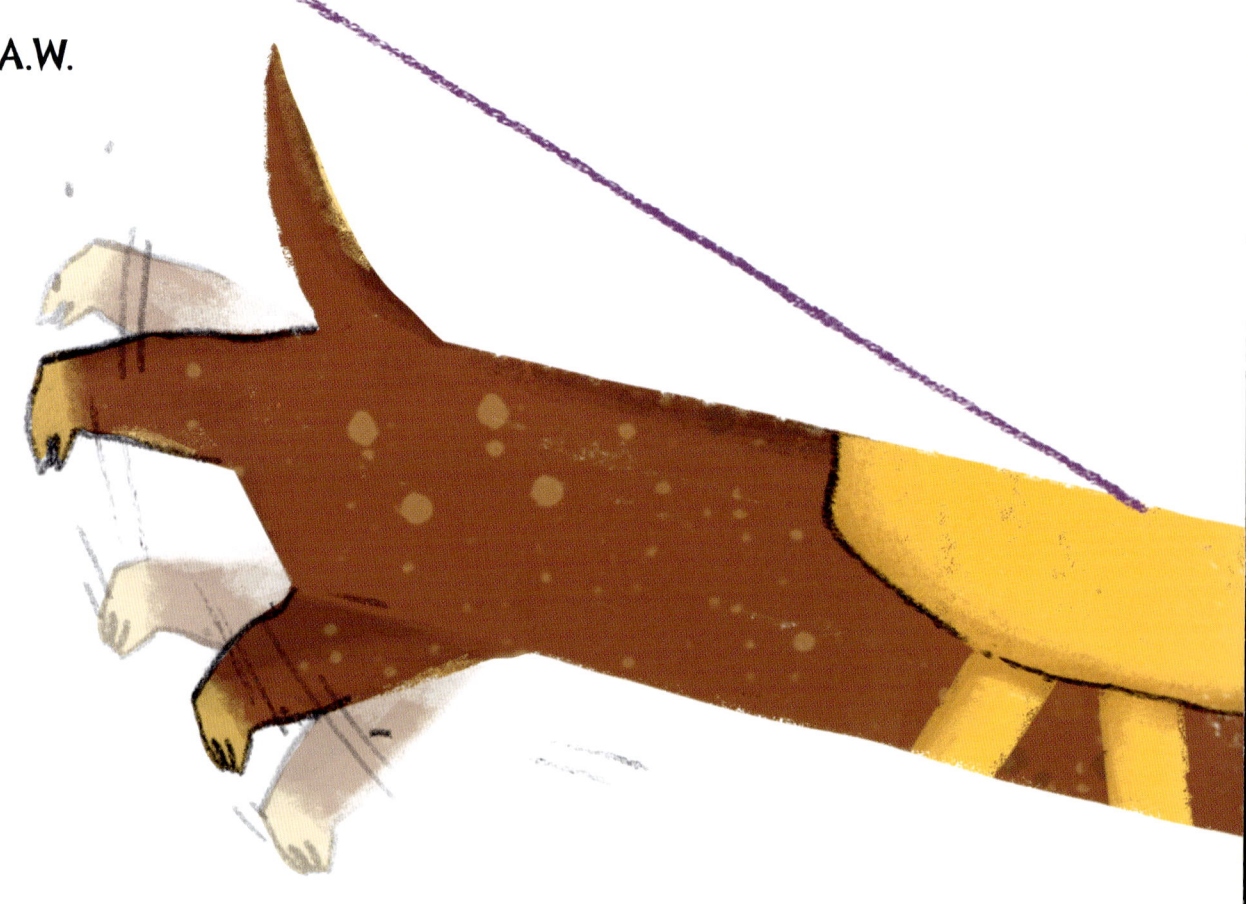

HODDER CHILDREN'S BOOKS

First published in Great Britain
in 2025 by Hodder & Stoughton

10 9 8 7 6 5 4 3 2 1

Text © Alastair Chisholm, 2025
Illustrations © Alex Willmore, 2025

The moral rights of the author
and illustrator have been asserted.

A CIP catalogue record for this
book is available from the
British Library.

ISBN 978 1 44497 7 738

Printed and bound in China

HODDER CHILDREN'S BOOKS
An imprint of Hachette Children's Group
Part of Hodder & Stoughton Limited
Carmelite House, 50 Victoria
Embankment, London EC4Y 0DZ

An Hachette UK Company

www.hachette.co.uk
www.hachettechildrens.co.uk

The authorised representative in the EEA is Hachette Ireland,
8 Castlecourt Centre, Dublin 15, D15 XTP3, Ireland
(Email: info@hbgi.ie)

MIX
Paper | Supporting
responsible forestry
FSC® C104740
FSC
www.fsc.org

Alastair Chisholm and Alex Willmore

ONE SILLY SAUSAGE DOG

Hodder
Children's
Books

What a **beautiful** sunny day!

Perfect for a walk in the park,
thinks Cordelia Sausage Dog.

The park is **EXCITING!**

And Cordelia is lovely, but not very sensible.
In fact, she is . . .

ONE SILLY SAUSAGE DOG!
"Oh!" she barks. "What's this?"

It's TWO bouncy bunnies,
hopping into rabbit holes.

Oh, that looks fun! thinks Cordelia.
I want to do that!

But she's still on her lead –
what's a sausage dog to do?

Then Cordelia has a clever idea.
She stretches...

and S T R E T C H E S...

THREE sparkly water fountains, shimmering in the sun. Cordelia stretches and jumps right in!

How refreshing!

"Oh, you **SILLY SAUSAGE DOG!**" wails her owner.

Oops! thinks Cordelia. **But what's THIS?**

It's **FOUR** whizzing bicycles, zooming to and fro!

"Race!" barks Cordelia.
"Race, race! Run, run, race!"

She stretches and races until her ears flap like flags.

What a **silly sausage dog!**

But then — **"What's this?"**

FIVE perfect sticks!

"I LOVE sticks!" barks Cordelia.
She stretches out and chomps . . .

ONE,

TWO,

THREE,

FOUR,

FIVE!

Look! **SIX** lost ducklings,
wandering on the grass.

"You should be in the pond,"
    says Cordelia.
"Don't worry, I'll help you!"

She tidies the ducklings away.
"I'm one *helpful* sausage dog," she says.

And then Cordelia **spies** . . .

NINE bouncing balls, boing, boing, boing!
"Got to catch them all!"

TEN frying sausages, sizzle, sizzle, sizzle!
"Is there one for me?"

Oh, there's so much to see, and do, and sniff!
And Cordelia is a **VERY** silly sausage dog,
and she can't help stretching . . .

and s t r e t c h i n g . . .

until she can't
S-T-R-E-T-C-H any more . . .

SPROIII

Cordelia springs all the way back!

"WOOF!"

she yelps, flying past all the things!

TEN frying sausages,
sizzle, sizzle, sizzle!

NINE bouncing balls,
boing, boing, boing!

EIGHT lovely
picnic baskets,
yum, yum, yum!

SEVEN dogs' bottoms,
sniff, sniff, sniff!

SIX lost ducklings,
quack, quack, quack!

FIVE perfect sticks,
chomp, chomp, chomp!

FOUR whizzing
bicycles,
race, race, race!

THREE sparkly water fountains, splish, splash, splosh!

TWO bouncy bunnies, hop, hop, hop!

And right back to where she started . . .

. . . ONE VERY SILLY SAUSAGE DOG!

"Cordelia, you naughty dog!" says her owner. "Look what you've done!"

Cordelia feels bad . . .

"I didn't mean it . . .

WAIT!"
she barks suddenly.

"I know what to do!"
She dashes off again, but this time . . .

she has a PLAN.

"You go here!" she barks.

"You stay there!"

"That way!"

"You down here!"

"You up there!"

"This way!"

"And . . . there!"

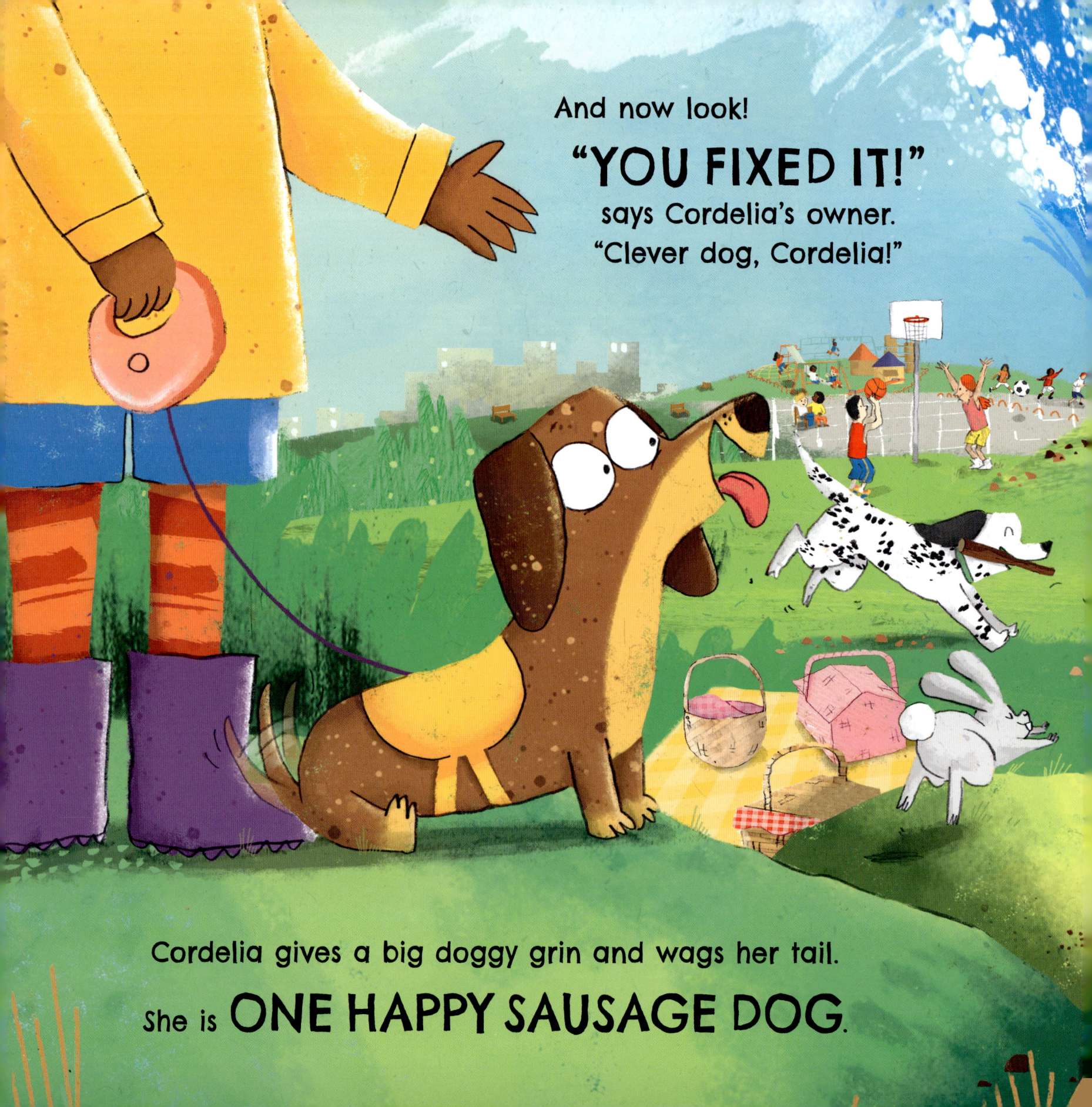

And now look!
"YOU FIXED IT!"
says Cordelia's owner.
"Clever dog, Cordelia!"

Cordelia gives a big doggy grin and wags her tail.
She is ONE HAPPY SAUSAGE DOG.

"Now, no more running off," says her owner. "Promise?"

"I promise," barks Cordelia.

And she means it. She really does . . .

OOH, BUT WHAT'S THIS?

"CAT!"

The End.